Family

cowboy boot

Grandma Thora

stuffed bunny

alarm clock

lollipop

suspenders

handkerchief

footstool

Grandpa Dave

pudding

oothpaste

doll carriage

baby bottle

rubber duckie

D.W.

toothbrush

Baby Kate

pacifier

For
Janet Schulman, F.C.E.
(first-class editor)

http://www.randomhouse.com/

Library of Congress Cataloging-in-Publication Data
Brown, Marc Tolon.
Arthur's really helpful word book / Marc Brown.
p. cm. SUMMARY: Uses labeled illustrations and
brief text showing Arthur and his family and friends at
the zoo, in the snow, in the kitchen, at Grandpa's farm,
and in other settings to present vocabulary words.
ISBN 0-679-88735-0 (trade) — ISBN 0-679-98735-5 (lib. bdg.)
1. Vocabulary–Juvenile literature. [1. Vocabulary.] 1. Title.
PE1449.B73 1997 428.1–dc21 96-54227

Printed in the United States of America
10 9 8 7 6 5 4 3 2 1

scissors

hairbrush

lizard

 pen

T-shirt

belt

birthday cake

zippers

pajamas

spaghetti

drum

undershirt

ARTHUR'S REALLY HELPFUL
Word Book

MARC BROWN

balloon

Random House New York

party hat

baby powder

telephone

anchor

recorder

beads

present

At Arthur's House

Saturday is clean-up day and everyone is busy. What are some of the things you can do to help around your house?

fireplace

roof

shutters

highchair

soap dish

towel

shower curtain

mirror

paintbrush

shampoo

door

faucet

toi

sink

tub

awning

staircase

pian

chair

telephone

chest

table

light switch

circuit breaker

steps

tools

dirty clothes

vise

workbench

o
c

light bulb

hot water heater

paint cans

matches

iron

needle & thread

ironing board

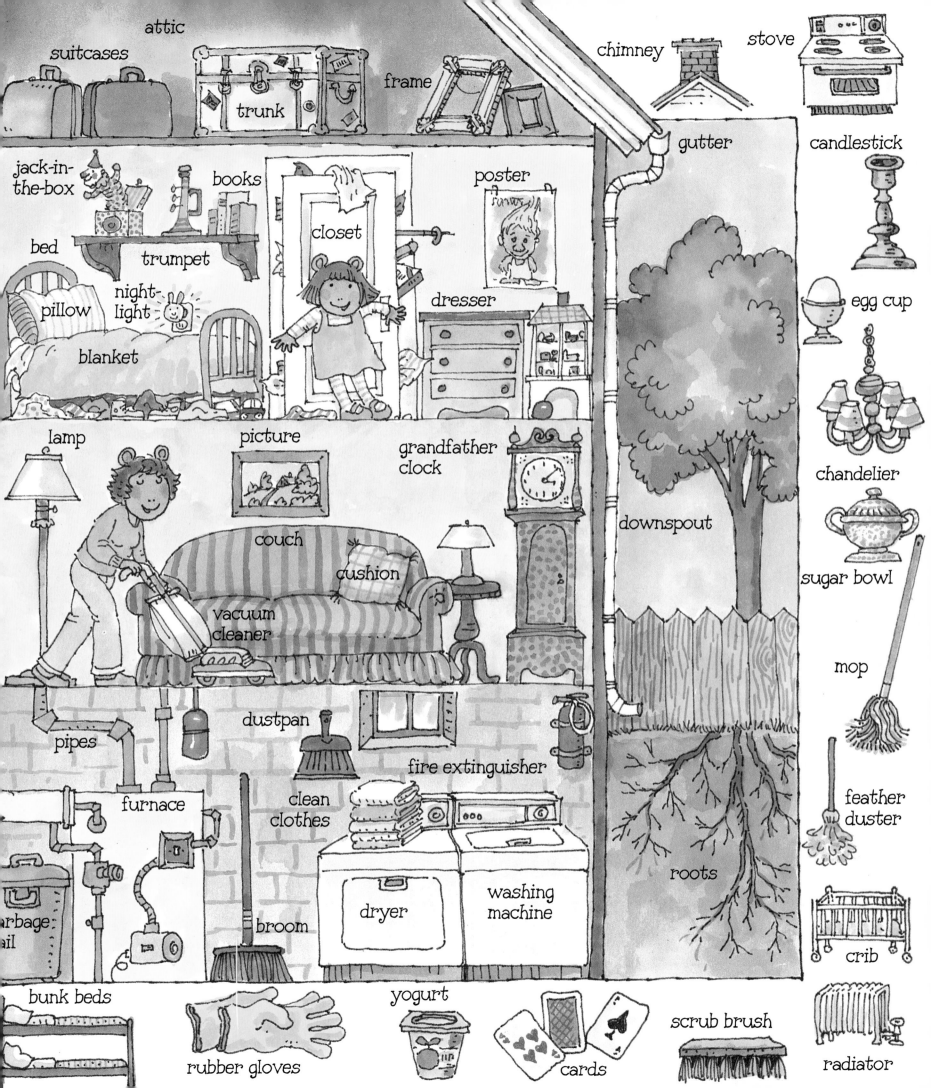

attic

suitcases

trunk

frame

chimney

stove

jack-in-the-box

books

poster

gutter

candlestick

closet

bed

trumpet

night-light

dresser

pillow

egg cup

blanket

lamp

picture

grandfather clock

chandelier

couch

downspout

sugar bowl

cushion

mop

vacuum cleaner

dustpan

fire extinguisher

pipes

clean clothes

feather duster

furnace

roots

garbage pail

broom

dryer

washing machine

crib

bunk beds

rubber gloves

yogurt

cards

scrub brush

radiator

deer

shark

elephant

crocodile

lion

At the Zoo

Watching the sea lions is always fun, but today there is some real monkey business going on at the zoo. All of the monkeys have escaped. Can you help the zookeeper find them?

zebra

giraffe

bird

ostrich

ticket booth

turnstile

zookeeper

panda

stroller

camel

dolphin

tiger

penguin

buffalo

leopard

hippopotamus

snake

parrots

hoop

fish

bucket

cardinal

ball

sea lion

turtle

balloons

gorilla

ICE CREAM

dog

anteater

polar bear

fox

peacock

At School with D.W.

Everyone is very busy at school today, including the class gerbil.
He likes stories too!

F funnel
G grasshopper
H houseboat
I igloo
J jellyfish
K kangaroo
L lock
M mermaid
N necktie
O orangutan
P piggy bank
Q queen
R rainbow

clock
paintings
storytime corner
story books
bookshelves
locks
teacher
liquid soap
fish food
fishbowl
juice
snack
crackers
toy cars

Counting

From 1 to 10 – can you count these city things?

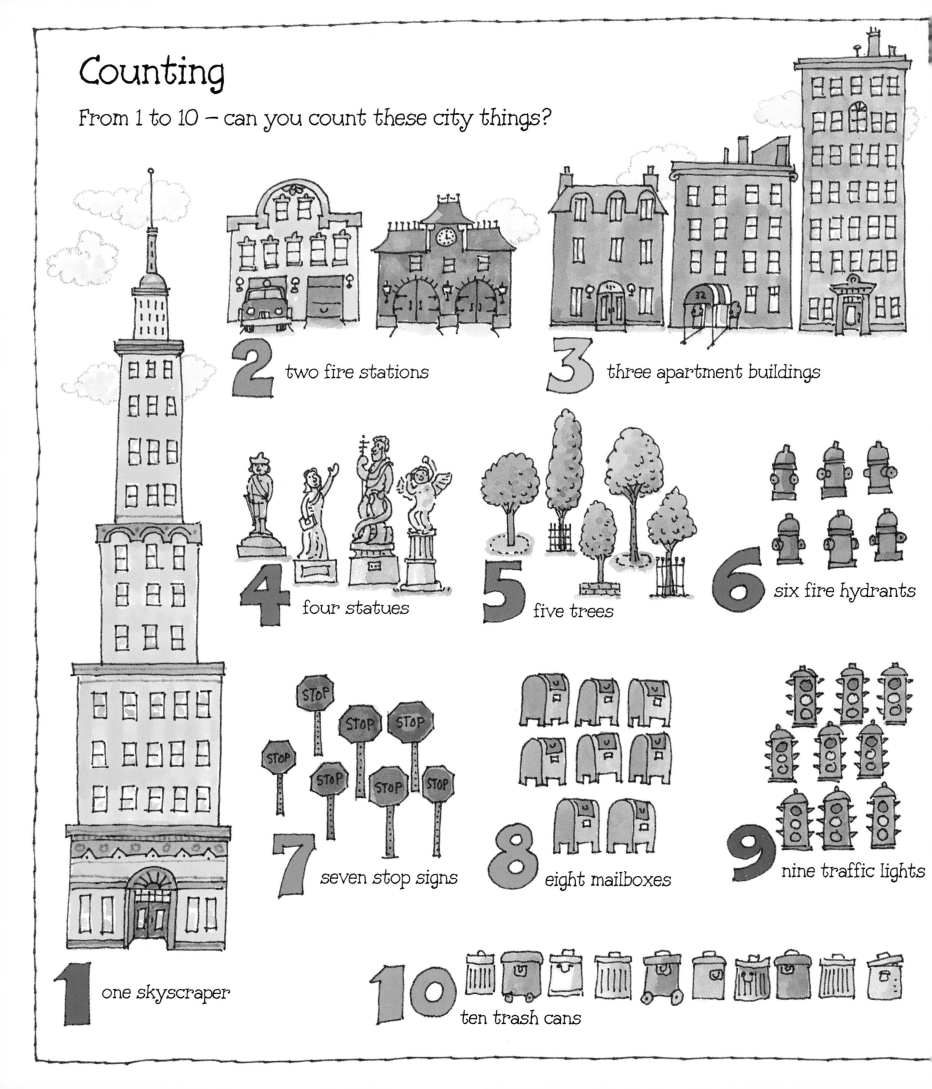

2 two fire stations

3 three apartment buildings

4 four statues

5 five trees

6 six fire hydrants

7 seven stop signs

8 eight mailboxes

9 nine traffic lights

1 one skyscraper

10 ten trash cans

Opposites

Do you know any others? Yes? No?

up   down   hot   cold   over   under

full   empty   asleep   awake   high   low

slow   fast   happy   sad   on   off

big   little   sweet   sour   young   old

The Big Bad Wolf

The Three Little Pigs

Little Red Riding Hood

Grandma

castle

sword

dragon

princess

Jack and the beanstalk

knight in armor

Storyland

Arthur loves to read stories.
He also likes to make up his own.
Would you like to make up a story?

GREAT STORIES

giant

Goldilocks

The Three Bears

Cinderella

prince

planet

antennae

alien

spacesuit

spaceship

gingerbread house

Hansel and Gretel

witch

Humpty Dumpty

flag

sails

ship

pirate

cannons

treasure chest

Tinker Bell

Peter Pan

At the Supermarket

Arthur has to do some shopping. Can you help him find everything on his list?

juice

peaches

ice cream

banana

raspberries

pear

lime

eggplant

peas

lettuce

toilet paper

MEAT

chicken

butcher

steaks

sausages

HOUSEHOLD

paper towels

BAKER

rolls

bread

cakes

cereal
pineapple
eggs
paper towels
bread

shopping ca.

apples

soap

flour

jam

celery

cucumber

batteries

tissues

lemon

cantaloupe

dish soap

tuna fish

kiwi

garlic

beet

mustard

orange

soda

SPECIAL

pineapples

bagels

CEREAL

muffins

DAIRY

butter

yogurt

soup

cheese

pie

milk

eggs

Swiss cheese

sauce

spaghetti

watermelon

pepper

gloves

snowball

cap

hockey stick

hockey puck

valentine

thermometer

icicles

snowflakes

snow shovel

bird feeder

fire hydrant

pipe

scarf

snowman

snowsuit

boots

mitten

Winter

It's a snowy day, and
the whole world is covered in white.
But there are some bright red things that stand out.
How many can you find?

blue jay

skis

poles

ice skates

goggles

earmuffs

toboggan

birdbath

gate

toad

mailbox

tricycle

roller skates

eggs

nest

triangle

square

chimney

roof

diamond

bone

circle

string

butterfly

rain hat

fence

helmet

raincoat

galoshes

bicycle

training wheels

umbrella

tulip

daffodil

crocus

robin

Spring

It is a beautiful day for flying kites and
having fun! These kites are all different shapes.
What shapes do you see?

puddle

snail

rake

hose

trowel

seeds

flowerpot

watering can

fan

ice cream truck

ice cream cone
ice cream pop

lobster

sunblock

sandals

Summer

A picnic at the beach is delicious on a hot summer day.
The ants think so too. How many ants came to
Arthur's picnic?

lighthouse

cliff

sailboat

motorboat

buoy

wave

dune

beach ball

beach bag

bathing suit

picnic basket

chips

shell

beach blanket

cup

sandwich

plate

gull

shovel

sand castle

pail

ants

starfish

lawnmower

sunglasses

beach umbrella

crab

pitcher

dandelion
seeds

Wampanoag Indians*

turkey

Pilgrim

moth

squirrel

acorn

wheelbarrow

branches

knife

window

leaves

tree

bush

happy   sad   surprised
jack-o'-lanterns

pumpkin

sweater

rake

Fall

D.W. is helping Arthur rake leaves.
Dad is getting ready for Halloween.
What kinds of faces did he carve?

*The Wampanoags were the Native Americans who attended the Pilgrims' first Thanksgiving.

football

gourds

witch

bat

ghost

cornstalks

mask

 bull

 cherries

 calf

 goose

 tomato

At Grandpa Dave's Farm

Arthur is learning how to milk a cow. The cow has something to say about that: Moooooooo! What do some of the other animals say?

Oink-oink

Moooooooo

pig

pigsty

cow

fly

tail

cowbell

Meow-meow

udder

cat   stool

pail

wheat

hoe

milk can

 mouse   horseshoe

hay wagon

 onions

watch

medicine

jellybeans

scale

shoes

French fries

television

popcorn

candy

dress

perfume

art supplies

BANK · ATM

CINEMA

NOW PLAYING
BIONIC BUNNY ON MARS
PRETTY PONY, COME HOME

Ice Cream Shop

escalator

TICKET BOOTH

OUT

IN

walkie-talkie

At the Shopping Mall

Arthur and D.W. agreed on a birthday present for their mom. But they can't agree on what movie to see. What movie do you think they should see?

security guard

pretzel

skirt

blouse

hair dryer

radio

soap

dice

video camera

basket

magazine

armchair

toaster

jeans

diamond ring

Bookstore

Toy Store

sundae

Jewelry

marionette

present

bracelet

necklace rings

dollhouse

robot

greeting card

bathrobe

pay telephone

fountain

bath brush

litter can

shopping bag

tennis racket

shorts

sled newspaper

underwear

milkshake

 train

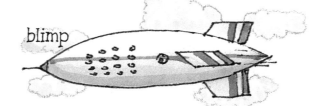 blimp

 submarine

Things That Go

What's your favorite way to get from here to there?

delivery van

Honk! Honk!

Renita's Flowers

Screech!

bicycle

RELIABLE MOVERS

Honk! Honk!

taxi

Beep! Beep! Beep! Bee

moving truck

TAXI

Whee-eeee! Whee-eee!

police car

Piccadilly Cir

POLICE

racing car

bulldozer

jeep

oil tank truck

swimming pool

star

lantern

duffel bag

compass

cooler

thermos

sleeping bag

first-aid kit

bug repellent

firewood

Backyard Camping

Telling spooky stories around the campfire can make you imagine all sorts of strange things. What do you see in the clouds?

clouds

smoke

marshmallows

log

water bottle

fire

flashlight

raisins

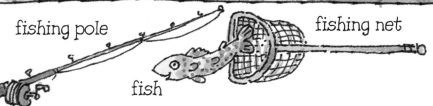
fishing pole

fish

fishing net

Ping-Pong paddle

Ping-Pong ball

tadpole

What's Inside?

Baby Kate has turned everything upside down. What a mess! Can you help Arthur and D.W. put everything back where it belongs?

toolbox

change purse

tissues

keys

pen

lipstick

comb

chewing gum

notebook

blocks

truck

teddy bear

doll

pull toy

yo-yo

lunchbox

screws

screwdriver

pliers

nails

hammer

drill

tape measure

pocketbook

cookie

carrot sticks

juice

sandwich

apple

napkin

toy chest

When Arthur Grows Up...

Here are some of the things he might be.

astronaut

fire fighter

police officer

cowboy

soldier

doctor

artist

rock star

teacher

chef

jester

construction worker

calculator

binder

marker

envelope

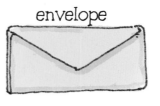

stamp

hole puncher

Mom at Work

Mom is an accountant. D.W. loves to visit her office. There are so many interesting things there, including a mouse that doesn't eat cheese. Can you find it?

lamp

pictures

bulletin board

cup

briefcase

TAXES

computer

telephone

important letters

drawer

desk

files

wastebasket

stapler

carpeting

paper clip

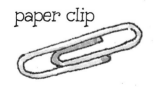

tape

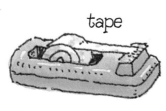

rubber bands

pencil sharpener

pushpin

eraser

thumbtack

wooden spoon

cookie cutters

measuring spoons

birthday candles

tongs

salt

pepper

timer

Dad at Work

Arthur's dad is a caterer. Sometimes Arthur helps him clean up.
He is very good at licking the spoons.

coffee

cooking oil

magnets

cupboard

microwave oven

dish soap

freezer

refrigerator

cake

sink

jam

pot

blender

mixing bowl

whisk

spatula

pastry bag

flour

rice

sugar

cake flour

dishwasher

pan

colander

tray

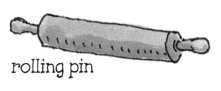

rolling pin

potholder

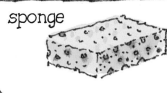

sponge

measuring cup

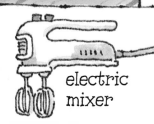

electric mixer

bench

dandelion

stream

bridge

swan

clover

pigeon

top

sweatshirt

rings

jungle gym

litter basket

At the Playground

D.W. is playing hide-and-seek and she is "it." Can you help her find Arthur, Muffy, Francine, and Binky? (Their pictures are on the last two pages.)

swings

...ready or not, here I come!

sand

sandbox

pail

grass

seesaw

pussywillow

jacks

spider

bandage

whistle

ladybug

slide

lunchbox

jump rope

lamppost

basketball hoop

bouncing ball

bell

ladder

basketball

playhouse

merry-go-round

squirrel

caterpillar

pogo stick

water lily

hopscotch game

sidewalk

sun

sand toys

trike

marbles

buttons

bottle caps

stamps

Diplodocus

Cetiosaurus

dolls

Collections

Buster has quite a collection of toy dinosaurs! People can collect all sorts of things. Do you have a collection?

marbles

pencils

caps

rocks

postcards

feathers

toy cars

coins

Stegosaurus

Triceratops

Allosaurus

shells

Tyrannosaurus rex

action figures

baseball cards

teddy bears